The History of Breathing

Allison Grimaldi Donahue

The History of Breathing

Sound Before Content

aktion_fiktion
DIAPHANES

If you want me to stay with you,
do not disperse your voice,
pitch it to the intimate moments.
Natalie Clifford Barney

I hear the high mezzo voice of the enigma.
Because it is the enigma: it doesn't explain itself,
it makes itself heard.
Hélène Cixous, *Tancredi Continues*

The rhythm of the painter should be like breaths
when life strangles us.
Maria Lassnig, *Ways of Being*

Infans infans without language. But a child cries in her attempt. Without your language which had become at once so personal and so public. They say we rely on pat phrases towards the end, the long end, years and years of fading without being able to name it as such. Clichés repeated at the tennis courts, running towards the net, unafraid expressions of aggression. The paradox of the self-projected self seems less important. The minor god comes down, a risky mission, and finally whispers in your ear and with a last hiccup something emerges, but it is without you. It doesn't take machines to make feelings on their own. A child's toy moos like a cow, a neon tube of acute notes whips through the air. A life-time of learning the ins and outs but you've already disappeared. The mouth speaks only for itself, an organ. No eloquent speeches or heartfelt apologies to lovers won and lost to children sired and raised. There is a shadow smiling, Cheshire Cat bearer of nonsense from the limerick to the anagram. But those too would re-quire much too much order, a pun like a hiccup to the frontal cortex. Years ago, a raspberry on the belly would have garnished such laughter but now only further sobs and cause for concern. Patients unable to perform other tasks can still thrust their tongues when observed, Doctor Rossi jots it down on her clipboard. What else then happens unobserved, what else are we all blind to. Like Morton Feldman wrote: Who but the dead know what it is to be alive? A cousin eating ice cream beside peaked toes out of a knit blanket wicked-witch style slurps atop the gift to be immediately handed down. I say, I see they leave their laundry everywhere and cups and plates and peanut butter-filled spoons that are always so hard to clean. It is both a churn and a clamoring tossing your head into a hamper with a gusty inhale. The flavors and the sensations on the tongue become a reminder of the way air travels so cold and burrowing through the body of course until it doesn't. A prayer made in silence with the mouth moving while you were lying on the airport floor in the darkness of the predawn. Nothing could be more youthful or full of life. There are sensations that you will never feel again long before now or then or when time no longer has any value to you. To you but to us yes, still, it lingers here, relentless in its authority. I'm looking through a window at water and ships and bridges and thinking of all you've missed already in such a short time. The perennial scene makes the present feel even less possible. Rifling through drawers as the documents and Polaroids of some past life it is too late to ask you directions to find. Sitting by the bed and scribbling my hand plays dead, too. Hypnagogia, the imagery that happens near sleep, is our illusion of leaving. The images behind eyelids though come from the most living unconscious depths, the activity that cannot be restrained. The truth is an immense majority of us die as we were born—oblivious. Nurse Flavia washed her and put on her pink nightgown. Propped up her rail thin body in the big green chair and turned on the *Teletubbies*. And she laughed and laughed and laughed. Remember the vindication of, I'll have the last laugh, muttered so many times at corporate meetings and mediations in glass towers and at her very late husband. This was her last night. In the dinosaur park I think of our bodies reconstructed bone by bone. It's coming to this, some sooner some later. In 500,000 years, the excavations will be quicker but by no means less mysterious. We are leaving the house the hallway and she pulls me to the corner. When Franco died, she says Tom put a tape recorder in the casket, it was voice activated, one of those old analog kinds. The next morning, he took it out before the other mourners arrived, before the mortician did a last check. It was Franco's voice, you know. And I don't really believe in that stuff, I don't but wouldn't a poet. If the god comes to visit you once he will visit you twice. Farinus, so boyish and so Roman, with his same face his same silly jumper, warm in embrace, one office for the doing and the undoing. Like in the municipal building, there only to communicate the greatest occasions. Nietzsche reminds us we're *der und der* when we die where is there where is that other there. It's the same in writing it's the same on the telephone. A whole life spent trying to be in two places at once will only leave you nowhere. Melly made a solemn pact that whichever of us should die first would endeavor to communicate with the other on the receiving end. I keep holding little seances by myself in the half hope half fear you're making the call.

GIOVANNI B. PERGOLESI.
(1710 - 1736)

The History of Breathing

My best theatrics are in the bedroom
8 am anger and 10 o'clock silence
the heavy breath of a secret

Opera is all about the power of release
trapped in a body I couldn't control
in a house that couldn't be mine
but still stands echoing lost memories

Its own lungs, so effortless, but me

I need a cure for nervousness and so
I am encouraged to stand before
an open window every morning
facing the trees and distant neighbors

to take deep breaths
to fondle my breasts
my rib cage.

Robert Frost once claimed that iambic pentameter is the most natural meter in which to write poetry, that it mimicked human voice. This was quickly contested by anyone and everyone writing in a language other than English, since, as we all know, every language has a different natural rhythm. We don't need analysis to teach us this, we know it, we hear it, we live it. But as we move through life something else happens, our rhythms and meters change, our capacity to hold a long note or shout to a distant friend diminishes. We develop our own systems of measurement and follow instinct that becomes rule. Words are made of meaning, but they are also simply utterances. That poetry is also sound and not just meaning, or rather the sounds of poetry reach beyond meaning. And as Charles Olson proposes, poetry's first goal may be to communicate meaning, but we shouldn't ignore its more magical, spiritual, curative second goal, to find a place in abstraction and experience in which we can reside.

This is the personal history of my poetic verse through my personal history of breathing: in singing lyrical opera, singing art songs. My fear of dying by not being able to get enough breath in my lungs. Not enough to finish a line and not enough to sing the end notes of this song.

Experience is dogmatic. We live something and then believe it to be true. The way we experience language in everyday life often feels dogmatic in meaning. Commands, instructions, dialogue with a certain level of expected coherence. But unlike everyday language, poetry invites us to experience logos fully, in our bodies, as point of action and reflection. American poet Charles Olson, wrote: “Art does not seek to describe but to enact.”

it was the humming, like a radiator shot across the room

it was my humming, a stream of invented song skimming the surface

you can't use words as ideas any more than that they can be strung as sounds. They are meanings only and actions of their own sort
                                        feelings and desires breath
the cause of words coming into existence

(Charles Olson)

it is my oldest memory, with the yellow walls, green chalkboard

it is my oldest memory, that my sounds are silenced

But I am convinced that personal memory and collective memory intertwine within us, to the point we can no longer distinguish the two. *Before man, before the invention of the ear, only the gods heard sounds.* (R. Murray Schafer, *The Soundscape)*

In the ancient Etruscan language, there were no spaces between written words. In the seventh and sixth centuries before Christ the words are continuous, a page has no empty space. There was only some limited punctuation to isolate consonants and vowels, but these were mostly used by teachers as a pedagogical tool. It is lightning outside, another hailstorm. I am in the museum and it is humid and rainy even from behind the windows. I stand before these three gold plates revising my own translation,

"this has been given to us, a sacred place for our goddess. We have been here for many years—as many as the stars."

I wander up the stairs and continue reading in what seems like the least popular corridor of the museum, "the correct sense of words is unknown." A language whose sounds and meanings remain elusive to us despite being part of our origins, humankind really hasn't existed for that long. I pause and think: what if the Etruscans took no breaths? Nothing in the exhibitions at Villa Giulia mention anything like that though. The writing of a people without pause, continuous sound, continuous silence; a man condemned to speech, a man condemned to his own chain of thoughts; inhales and exhales like paragraphs underwater. The question of the space between the words, what happens in the gaps and breaks and moments of seeming nothingness. Men like Eric Garner, choked into nothingness, chests compressed, when the last words aren't the words anyone is looking for. I think of Giles Corey, and the misguided notion that you can push a confession out of an innocent man through his windpipe. Of Tarpeia under her jewels, of Margaret Clitherow under 700 pounds of stone, of Roman traitors under elephant's foot, I think of Eric Garner and his loosie cigarettes. I think what rhythms his poem would have.

dip yr hand into the rocks
to feel the heaves
hot breath like vulcan
like an old man dying
a force which goes unmeasured
is no force at all

Olson wrote that there are two sorts of poets: those concerned with the choice of individual words and those concerned with how words relate to one another. I fall into the second group. Alone my words mean nothing, they form relationships not only of meaning but sound and occupancy. In the Etruscan world where would I stand? The utterance was sacred and wasn't transcribed. The two languages, written and spoken, were different, as they were for so many ancient cultures. It is a world I cannot imagine—me, with all of my staccato sounds. A few years ago I was translating a poet who uses entire blank pages to imply a long breath. Those Etruscans would have thought her so wasteful.

In Pyrgi, now Santa Severa, we go to the beach in July. It is the weekend and we eat eggplant sandwiches and sweat under the sun. In Pyrgi they found the bilingual Phoenician and Etruscan plates. If we dig deep, for sea glass and shells, could we also find language?

Soprano
A - ma - ril - li mia bel - la, no cre - di'o del mio cor dol -
BC
S
- ce de - si - o, d'es - ser tu l'a - mor mi - o?
BC

—for Chantal Akerman

a fold is that which I cannot see
under the guise of flesh and commonplace
the weight of teeth and tongue

a backgammon court crumbling
outside crows stamp on hard plastic
a fold is that which I cannot see

a sponge bath glaze without dignity
seashells left beside your pillowcase
the weight of teeth and tongue

fat collects under my fingernails
there is no longer anyone to plead my case
a fold is that which I cannot see

an act like a bee sting
paper cuts almost never come from lace
the weight of teeth and tongue

if there's an aura, hand it to me
the flowers in the garden grow at an unending pace
a fold is that which I cannot see
the weight of teeth and tongue

In my family there was no poetry, but there was song. There was eating and there was song. A band of illiterates feasting on their young. Werner Heisenberg, theoretical physicist, wrote: "He who possesses rhythm possesses the universe." So, what else did we need? All of our dreams were caught up in our breathlessness. All of *our* dreams *are* caught up in our breathlessness. When I was young my mother placed those dreams on me and had me taking piano and dancing lessons. Then they discovered I had a big lung capacity, I liked to sing along to *Annie* and they sent me to singing lessons. I'm still not sure why I agreed to it, I'm still not sure if I disliked it. The puzzle of distinguishing childhood dreams from those who raised us.

Voice.
p
cresc.
Seb - ben, cru - de - le, mi fai lan - guir, sem - pre 'e -
Tho' not de - serv - ing Thy cru - el scorn, Ev - er un -
p
cresc.
più cresc.
rit.
de - le, sem - pre fe - de - le ti vo - glio a - mar.
swerv - ing, ev - er un - swerv-ing Thee on - ly I love.
più cresc.
rit.

Charles Olson in his essay "Human Universe" writes: "We have lived long in a generalizing time, at least since 450 B.C. And it has had its effects on the best of men, on the best of things. Logos, or discourse, for example, in that time, so worked its abstractions into our concept and use of language that language's other function, speech, seems so in need of restoration that several of us go back to hieroglyphs or to ideograms to right the balance. (The distinction here is between language as the act of the instant and language as the act of thought about the instant.)" Language as act, language as reflection, a double imperative.

The task of the poet is to write the instant. To transcribe what is happening now, in this very moment. I have found I am often at odds with how I thought poets should compose work. My disregard for set forms of meter and rhyme, my fixation on other rules, my bursts of writing, it all makes me feel like a fraud. And then of course, it isn't that I have a disregard for meter and rhyme, but rather, I have my own way of feeling them out. It comes down to the sounds things make. The things of language, how the different phonemes fit in my mouth, how I imagine them in the minds and mouths of others, repeating, changing. As a child I did study music but I haven't sung in public since I joined a Bach Chorus in Freiburg during a year studying abroad in 2005. There, I learned how to hold sounds and words inside for a given amount of time in unison, each syllable a measure, a breath, in a language I could barely speak. Poetry, the revered, ancient and too often feared genre is nothing more than holding the breath of words for a given amount of time. I could play with the German language with complete disregard for content. I would walk around reciting and memorizing guttural sounds. In my family no one was writing poems, but they were hissing and yelling and singing and sighing, people were exasperated and aspirated and speaking through running water, salt burning in your eyes, a contest in pain and lung capacity.

frost heaves and pneumonia
when i cry mucus gathers across my lips
slime up like split grapes
grates to the underground
toothy soul

how much is required to make one syllable
clear if not poignant just for today
a chorus of trees or the option
of collective absorption
breath as pause
breath as time signature
breath as dog's breath
last breath
heavy breather
movie theater creeper
destination fog from the backseat
                                        window

When I first sang those songs with my piano teacher in high school, I didn't know what they meant. I worked on mispronouncing Italian diligently, my mother attentive and excited and committing each song to memory. My grandmother would cry. What if we walked around just howling to one another. Years later, at my mother's funeral I see my grandmother, in fact, as she howls into the casket. She doesn't understand the words to Schubert's *Ave Maria* either, but she kneels and collapses and yelps, and after years without practice I decided I will sing for her again. A singing machine to make my grandmother proud. Something clear and definable and so goddamn feminine.

holding notes
holding feelings

I become obsessed with Cecilia Bartoli. It's the art songs that I love. From Italy in the 16th and 17th and 18th centuries. The songs require a delicate voice, attention to diction. I stand in front of the mirror and sing recitatives and arias, song with ABA strophic structures about heartbreak and abandon. My favorites are always the ones with abandon. Women tossing themselves from bridges for love. And then it turned out I'm a lesbian. And it turns out, if you're a lesbian, your primal scene must involve song. I slept with an opera singer one summer in college. We carried on an affair in a small mountain town where we were studying German. She would sing evenings at the white clapboard Episcopal church and afterwards I'd make her come in my bedroom overlooking the Green Mountains. In my mind it becomes more and more early 20th century; idyllic New England romance. It was a disaster.

Paul Celan: *Atemwende*, turning of our breath
it's all air and nerves, this vibrato no one wants
i go to german school to learn the ablative but
emerge with a corpulent soprano
a lover outside the body and not of it

Linguist Otto Jespersen writes, "Although we now regard the communication of thought as the main object of speaking, ... it is perfectly possible that speech has developed from something which had no other purpose than that of exercising the muscles of the mouth and throat and of amusing oneself and others by the production of pleasant or possibly only strange sounds." Aliens arrive on Earth to hear our melodic whispers. Would they not find it beautiful?

And we are not certain, which comes first, which comes second. Why one thing is better than the next. But it is certain that content is continually overrated. I want a poem to lull me. I want a poetry to collapse the distinction between all forms of logic.

Olson again:

"I take it that PROJECTIVE VERSE teaches, is, this lesson, that that verse will only do in which a poet manages to register both the acquisitions of his ear *and* the pressure of his breath."

"And together, these two, the syllable *and* the line, they make a poem, they make that thing, the—what shall we call it, the Boss of all, the 'Single Intelligence.' And the line comes (I swear it) from the breath, from the breathing of the man who writes, at the moment that he writes, and thus is, it is here that, the daily work, the WORK, gets in, for only he, the man who writes, can declare, at every moment, the line its metric and its ending—where its breathing, shall come to, termination."

If I keep singing, the lines will extend, the words will increase in syllables. I speak Italian all day to find my English is baroque, I make a phone call to an old friend and she asks why I use such old-fashioned words. At a bar in Brooklyn someone tells me I am speaking with an accent.

the blessing of the throat
candlesticks only lighted in my mind
melting quickly around my neck
the felty church carpet
the stale smell of my faith

On my last visit home to Connecticut I go to visit my aunt. This is my mom's sister; she's four years younger than my mother would have been, but now she's outlived her. We are sitting at her kitchen table. I am sitting in a chair. She is sitting in a very complicated electric wheelchair. Like my mother, she has Amyotrophic lateral sclerosis, ALS, sclerosi laterale amiotrofica, SLA in Italian. Lou Gehrig's disease. The elaborate chair gives her a real Stephen Hawking vibe, except my aunt was a hairdresser and wasn't so interested in the life of the mind as much as the life of the body, life of the heart. She enjoyed her body, its strength, its ability to move and bend and work. She was always taking on new projects, renovations, keeping busy, painting walls, digging gardens. Now she laughs in her chair. A continuous, unstoppable laughter at something I've said, or something one of her young grandchildren has done. When this first starts happening, it seems like part of her personality that has always been there. The laughing, the element of joy. Then I learn it is because once she starts she can't stop, and in reality it is quite dangerous, her laughter could choke her.

keep it here beneath the bed
where i have to pull it out
covered in dust i am coughing now
you are coughing now and pulling at
the waffle blanket and at its combs
each of them filled
with something invisible

bulb in the beeker
disproportionate sucking in
to the sucking out
one two three four
pushes measured in centimeters
and seconds i don't remember
one two three four
how we disposed of the evidence
left at the curbside goodwill
or in the basement boxes

when speech turns to laughter
and the mechanism goes—

the joke is over
in yr lazy-boy lungs

laughter with an accomplice
bones grow long
and like a milkshake
spilled across the tongue

I would watch her mouth as she ate, my mother, watch her hands as she clawed at the lobster, still managing to extract more meat than anyone else at the dinner table. It remains one of her finest scenes. In the late summer of 2012. The last summer and she was still strong. My girlfriend and I had just come back from a camping trip in Vermont. She sits at the head of the table making jokes about herself for company, telling us she would rather die than live like this. "The carnivores produce the greatest range of individual sounds..." (R. Murray Schafer, *The Soundscape)*

A flashback to better times. To 2002. We eat a plate of spaghetti and meatballs and set out on our journey. It is a six- hour ride and we have *Jesus Christ Superstar,* Andrew Lloyd Weber's magnum opus, on repeat. Oh, the sounds. Schafer again: "In the *Phaedrus,* Plato has Socrates tell how the cicadas were originally men who were touched by the muses so that they devoted their lives to singing and, forgetting to eat, died to be reborn as insects."

Voice.
p
Pur di - ce - sti, o boc - ca, boc - ca bel - la, o
Mouth so charm - ful, O tell me now, O tell me, O
sempre p
boc - ca, boc - ca bel - la, quel so - a - ve e
tell me now, O tell me Why thy sweet - ness

My mother and I have the air. Swooping down from the third-floor apartment on slack rope last night's laundered garments skimming the dust. Old solutions for old problems. It never gets old—to admit yr wrong as seasons change and arms and legs stay stiff late into the morning.

My mother and I speak through the air. See: nothing's changed. Bachelard: *air brings nothing. It gives nothing. It is the immense glory of nothing.* So we still sit here with nothing between us. What a lie. If it is such a nothing, why is my longing so strong? Why do my eyes burn? Why is the fog so thick?

My mother could hold her breath for so many minutes, how many now is completely lost to me. It was so long. She had so many talents, but this one proved something to me as a child. I wanted to be like her. Blue in the face. If this disease is genetic, I can only I hope I too will die laughing.

Willa Cather in *The Song of the Lark* writes: "No matter how long a breath you have, the storm has a longer." It proves itself right so suddenly. The only muscle both controlled and uncontrolled. In our voice we give birth and we kill, in our voices we set free our ghosts. Cather again: "Voices are so often disappointing; especially women's voices. So much chance about it, so many factors. ... Perhaps that is why they interest one. All the intelligence and talent in the world can't make a singer. The voice is a wild thing. It can't be bred in captivity. It is a sport, like the silver fox. It happens." That's what happened to me. Not that I had the discipline or the talent, but mostly I think I was tame. Withholding even to myself, and not only about my voice. Instead of continuing the song, I shut down the song; maybe if I'd kept singing, it would have all come rushing out. Brenda Hillman writes in her poem "Street Corner" that "words are breath bricks." I hurl them all at my mother. And at my father. In my twenties I stop singing, start smoking. As my mother's ALS progresses, I hold it against her, those muscles she can't use. It may also have to do with my coming out, with my fear of coming out.

Wayne Koestenbaum, *The Queen's Throat*: "Only after puberty can a singer place the voice, discover where chest voice ends and head voice begins; only then can the singer balance the irreconcilable symbolic values of the head and chest."

Me and my anxiety. I didn't sing at her funeral. Could I have managed? It would have been the most fitting tribute. My mother dies and I take up the instrument she longed to play. The accordion. It is all breath. Like in my head, the music jingle jangles alone in a hollowed-out space. Private sound cavern of the modern man. I transfer my complicated voice into another complicated corpus, not in my body but of it.

Massenet's *Sapho* playing in the background as we begin.

No, rather: Ethel Smyth, *The Wreckers.*

The main character is Fanny Legrand: a great name.

it stops

the blue lights are where no windpipes blow
and the dinging of soft but broken clocks
keeping time has always been our fancy
female Orpheus
a literally unsexed "fourth" voice for a "third" sex

"singing is a stream," Lilli Lehmann told singing pupils
but when then, do we lift our heads and gasp the air?

—for Maria Lassnig

A voice is located in its history
Breathe in, it's an idea
I write myself as a fallen angel

Continually I answer, continually I am transformed
Ransacked and criminal
A voice is located in its history

These fingers drew these bovines
Weaving and worship, weaving and worship
I write myself as a fallen angel

A diadem remains nestled in
Green gardens of abandon
A voice is located in its history

Cut the throat to find flowing locks
The bulls stare, quizzical
I write myself as a fallen angel

My merry-go-round spins off its base
Wasps the size of hummingbirds
A voice is located in its history
I write myself as a fallen angel

GIUSEPPE GIORDANI. (GIORDANELLO.)
(1743 - 1798.)
Larghetto. (♩ = 60.)
Piano.
dolce.
largamente.
p
Ca - ro mio ben, cre - di - mi al - men, sen - za di te lan - guisce il
Thou, all my bliss, Be - lieve but this: When thou art far My heart is
p dolce.
cor_ ca - ro mio ben, sen - za di te_ lan - gui - sce il
lorn._ Thou, all my bliss, When thou art far_ My_ heart_ is
f
p

Look in this jar
see the larynx see
your voice

Se tu m'ami, se sospiri
(If thou lov'st me.)

Arietta.

English Version by
Dr. TH. BAKER.

GIOVANNI B. PERGOLESI.
(1710 - 1736)

a tempo
che_so-let-to Io_ti-deb-ba ri - a-mar, Pa-sto-rel - lo, sei sog-get-to
that demure-ly I_on thee a - lone_may smile, Simple shepherd, thou art sure-ly
a tempo
pp
cresc.
Fa - cil-mente a t'in-gannar; Pa-sto-rel-lo, sei sog-get-to Fa - cil-men-te a
Prone thy sens-es to beguile; Simple shepherd, thou art surely Prone thy senses_
p
cresc.
p
t'in-gan-nar, Fa - cil - men - te a_ t'in-gan-nar. Bel-la ro-sa
to be-guile, prone thy_ sens - es_ to be-guile. As a fair red
p
poco cresc.
por-po - ri - na Og - gi Sil-via sce-glie - rà, Con la scu - sa
rose, a_lov-er Fain might Sil-via choose to - day, Hap-ly if_ he

sempre cresc.
del - la spi - na Do - man poi la sprez - ze - rà, Doman poi la sprez - ze - rà.
thorns dis - cov - er 'Tis to - morrow thrown a - way, 'Tis to - mor - row thrown a - way.
sempre cresc.
cresc. un poco
Ma de - gli uomi - ni il con - si - glio Io per me non se - gui - rò. Non perchè mi
All men say of maid - en - fol - ly Finds no fa - vor in mine eyes, Nor because I
cresc. un poco
rit.
pia - ce il gi - glio Gli al - tri fio - ri sprez - ze - rò.
love the lil - y Shall I oth - er flow'rs de - spise.
a tempo
rit.
p
p
cresc.
Se tu m'a - mi, se tu so - spi - ri Sol per
If thou lov'st me, and sigh - est ev - er But for
p
cresc.

rit.
p a tempo
me, gen-til pa - stor, Ho do-lor de' tuoi mar-ti-ri, Ho di-let-to
me, O gen-tle swain, Sweet I find thy lov-ing fa-vor, Pi-ti-ful I
rit.
p a tempo
f rit.
del tuo a-mor, Ma se-pen-si che so-let-to Io ti deb-ba ri - a-mar,
feel thy pain. Should'st thou think tho', that de-mure-ly I on thee a-lone may smile,
f rit.
a tempo
pp
Pa-sto-rel-lo, sei sog-get-to Fa-cil-mente a t'in-gannar, Pa-sto-rel-lo,
Simple shepherd, thou art sure-ly Prone thy sens-es to beguile; Simple shepherd
a tempo
p
cresc.
rit. assai
sei sog-get-to Fa-cil-mente a t'in-gannar, Fa-cil-mente a t'in-gannar.
thou art sure-ly Prone thy sens-es to beguile, prone thy sens-es to beguile.
rit. assai
cresc.

The text was developed and performed in different versions at Sant'Andrea Scaphis Rome in 2019 and Kunsthalle Bern in 2022.

First printing 2025

Dresdener Strasse 118, 10999 Berlin

kontakt@diaphanes.net · www.diaphanes.net

Layout: 2edit, Zurich

Printed in Germany

ISBN 978-3-0358-0833-9